From Seeds to Trees Press
FromSeedsToTreesPress.com

ISBN: 979-8575721192 (Paperback)

From Seeds to Trees Press provides special discounts when purchased in larger volumes for premiums and promotional purposes, as well as for fundraising and educational use. Custom editions can also be created for special purposes. For more information, please visit our website at FromSeedsToTreesPress.com

Oh, the Seeds You Can Sow

Written by
Jessica Lisk

Illustrated by
Gabby Correia

# Hi There!

My name is Janie Grace, and boy, do I have a story
to tell you! It's an epic tale, full of
adventure and magical powers.

Ok, not really.

But, it's still a pretty spectacular story, I think, and
if it's put into the right hands, it could very well
change the world.

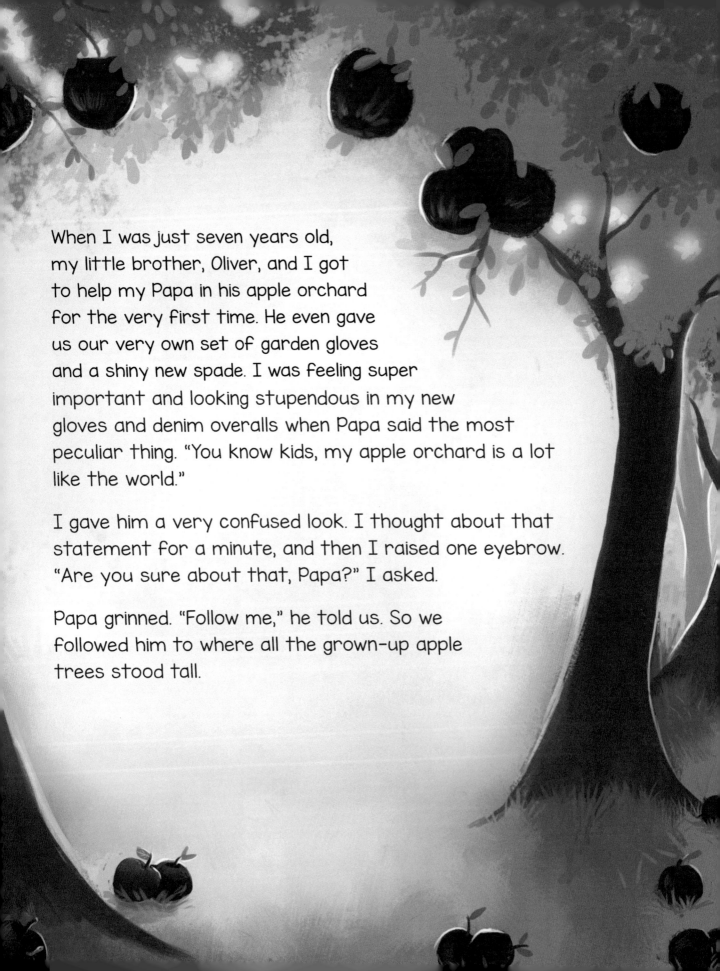

When I was just seven years old,
my little brother, Oliver, and I got
to help my Papa in his apple orchard
for the very first time. He even gave
us our very own set of garden gloves
and a shiny new spade. I was feeling super
important and looking stupendous in my new
gloves and denim overalls when Papa said the most
peculiar thing. "You know kids, my apple orchard is a lot
like the world."

I gave him a very confused look. I thought about that
statement for a minute, and then I raised one eyebrow.
"Are you sure about that, Papa?" I asked.

Papa grinned. "Follow me," he told us. So we
followed him to where all the grown-up apple
trees stood tall.

He reached up and picked a pretty red apple, then took a small knife from his pocket and cut it open. "See these tiny black seeds?" he said. I nodded.

"'Course I do," I told him. Oliver must not have seen them because just then, he started digging in the dirt for bugs.

"How many seeds do you see?" I counted. "Six."

"How many apples?"

I laughed at him a little. "There's only one apple, silly.

"Are you sure?" he asked.

"Positive," I said proudly.

"Well, what if I plant each of these six seeds, and they grow up to be trees that make apples? *Now* how many apples do I have in my hand?"

I looked at those six little seeds and thought about that one real hard. "Hmm... well, I guess we don't know for sure, but it could be a whole bunch." I said.

Papa smiled at me. "Right, because not only will those trees make lots of apples, but those apples will also have seeds. And if you plant those seeds, they'll make even more apples."

"Wow!" I told him. "That is a lot of apples!" I wrinkled my face up a little. "But I still don't understand how seeds and apples are like the world."

He took us back to the greenhouse. "Let's get to work planting, and I'll explain what I mean," he said. So I got busy filling pots with the moist, black soil while Oliver unstuffed his pocket full of worms. And that's when Papa told me the part that changed my life forever.

"Every time we say things or do things to other people, we are planting seeds in their hearts, and they don't even know it. We can plant good seeds or bad seeds. And whatever kind of seed we plant will produce that same kind of fruit on the outside." He showed me the apple seeds again.

"Oh, the seeds you can sow in this world, Janie Grace, if you just look for the opportunities. And every time you say or do something kind, you are planting good seeds in someone else's heart."

My face lit up all of a sudden. "And then, they can plant the seeds of their fruit in someone else's heart too! Right, Papa?"

"That's right!" Papa said. "You never know how far just one little seed will go." I smiled real big. I wasn't sure how much of a difference just one little girl could make. I knew it was a great big world with lots and lots of people, and I probably didn't have enough seeds to go around, but I was excited to give it all I had.

"Oh, and Janie Grace," he said, "some seeds need a bit more watering than others, so don't ever get discouraged. You just keep planting those good seeds, and remember, a little bit of water goes a long way."

The next day at school, I was determined to do some seed planting. I walked right up to my teacher, Mrs. O'Grady, gave her one of Papa's red apples and told her, "You look extra lovely today, ma'am." When I turned around to go back to my seat, I did a little smirk because I had planted a good seed right in her heart and she didn't even know it.

Next, when my best friend, Molly, got a bad grade on her report card and started to cry, I spotted another opportunity to plant a seed. I patted her on the shoulder and simply told her, "It's ok. You'll do better next time!"

Then later, during math class, I got a teensy bit bored. So, I tore off a small piece of paper and wrote in my neatest handwriting, "You are awesome. Pass it on." I crumpled it up and passed it to the kid sitting beside me who I had never heard speak a single word in my whole life.

I smiled at him real big as he opened it. He just stared at me for a minute. "Um. Thanks," he finally said. "You are most welcome," I said back to him in my most polite voice. "Now go ahead, pass it on," I reminded him.

So he did.

And so did the next person. And guess what? That little tiny seed of a paper went so far that it went all the way to the principal's office and planted itself right on her desk. She scolded me for passing notes in class, but I like to think that secretly, she needed to feel awesome too.

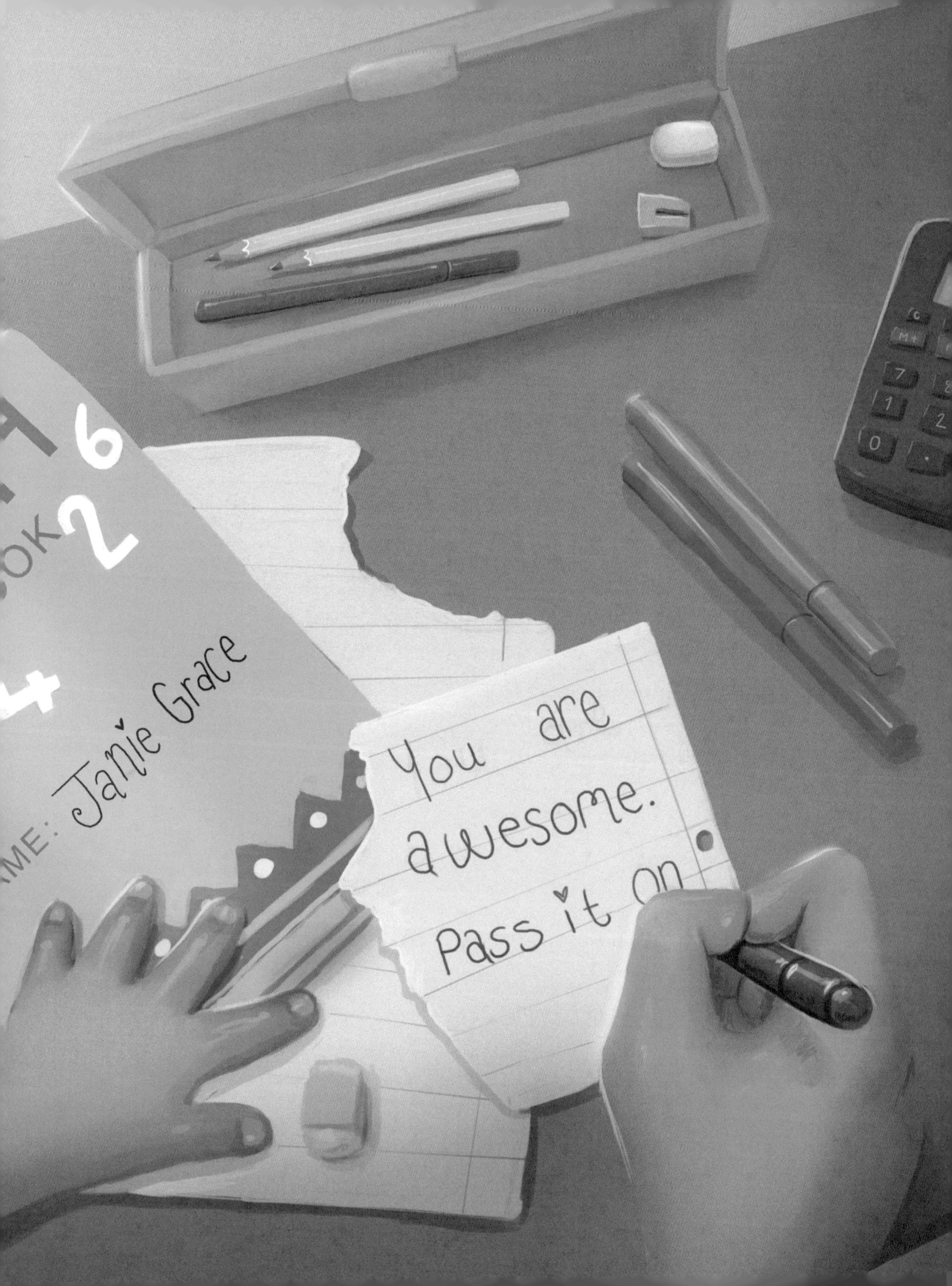
6
OK 2
4
AME: Janie Grace
You are
awesome.
Pass it on

When I was on the way back to class, I saw the Big Bad Bully Boy, Brady Bradford.

Well, that's what I called him anyway.

He hated school, so he was always goofing off and bullying people. He was always getting into trouble. I noticed him picking up trash around the school lots of days, but that day I felt sort of bad for him. I knew he never would've offered to help me, but I thought that just maybe he needed a good seed planted in his heart.

So, I marched right up to him and said, "I'll help!" We worked together for a while, and he was so shocked by my seed planting, I think, that he didn't even say a word. Not even "thank you". But I remembered what Papa had said about not getting discouraged, so I decided that I would water that seed a little more later.

On the way home from school, we stopped to get a few groceries from the supermarket, and I noticed that the cashier was a little under the weather. Sometimes, I have a bad habit of letting any thought that pops into my head just fly right out of my mouth, but I most certainly could not tell him that he looked awful.

That definitely would've been a bad seed.

I thought about how exhausting it must have been to stand there scanning so many people's things while feeling icky. I gave him a big smile. "Hey sir, I'm sorry you're not feeling well," I said, "here's a tissue and a juice box." I was sure that Mother didn't even mind that I shared a few items out of our grocery cart, and plus, I was very proud of that sneaky little seed I planted right into that guy's heart.

That night, I was busy working hard on my project, so I told Oliver that I couldn't help him build robots. He had what Mom calls an outburst and threw a block right at my head. I gritted my teeth a little and thought about planting a seed of anger right into his face, but then I slowly let out a long breath and said, "Ok Ollie. It's very rude to throw things, but I will play with you for just a little while. Ok?"

Every day after that, I decided to plant some new seeds and water some old ones. It took a while, but guess what? I started seeing good fruit everywhere, because people were starting to pass it on, of course.

Mrs. O'Grady started an official Compliment Club. Students were given a special invitation to the club when they were caught giving a compliment to a classmate.

Molly worked really hard to bring her grades up, and she even started helping others with their homework too.

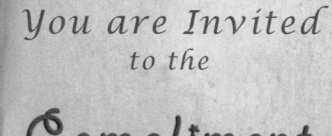

You are Invited
to the

Compliment
Club

Congratulations!
you are awesome

Oh, and you'll never believe what happened with that sneaky little note. Somehow, it made it all the way to the 6 o'clock news! I knew that Principal McPipkin would pass it on! Sneaky seed planter. And one night when my dad came home feeling sick, he said, "The nicest thing happened to me today. I stopped by the supermarket for some cold medicine, and the cashier gave me some tissues and a juice box- no charge!" I just smiled at him super big.

Oliver even started to plant some good seeds too, and I knew deep down inside that it had all started with my tiny little seeds.

Today, I am Mrs. Janie Grace. I am all grown up now, but I tell this story to a new set of children every single year. I tell them to plant good seeds and not bad ones. I tell them not to get discouraged and to continue to water the good seeds they've planted even if they don't see fruit for a long time. I tell them that they never know how far one seed will go or how many apples can come from just one seed.

And every single year, someone will ask, "What happened to the bully, Brady Bradford?" I just smile and say "Oh, Mr. Bradford? He's your principal."

Then later, I'll take a drive out to Papa's old apple orchard, because it always reminds me to never underestimate the magical power of planting one tiny seed – it could very well **change the world!**

Papa's Just-the-Right-Size Apple Pies

What You Will Need:

- 2 cookie sheets
- 4in. cookie cutter (Papa uses a Mason jar lid, but I prefer heart-shaped.)
- Parchment paper or a silicone mat
- 2 boxes store-bought pie crust (4 crusts)
- 1 21 oz. can apple pie filling
- 4 tbsp butter, softened
- Cinnamon and sugar
- Vanilla and/or caramel extract
- 1 c. powdered sugar
- 2-4 tbsp milk
- A whole bunch of love

1. Allow pie crusts to sit at room temperature for about 15 minutes. Preheat the oven to 375 . Line cookie sheets with parchment paper or silicone mats.

2. Carefully unroll the pie crusts on a floured or non-stick surface. Use a cookie cutter to cut as many shapes out as possible. Re-roll any remaining dough and cut again. Space half of the crust shapes out on lined cookie sheets.

3. Using a fork or butter knife, mix the apple pie filling as to mash the larger pieces of apple into smaller bits. Spoon about 1 tbsp of filling onto each crust shape. Lay remaining crust shapes directly on top of the filled crusts, making a pocket. Use a fork to crimp the outer edges of each pie.

4. In a small bowl, melt 3 tbsp of the butter, reserving 1 tbsp for later. Mix in cinnamon and sugar to taste. Add a splash of vanilla or caramel extract. Brush mixture over top of each sealed pie. Bake for 25-30 minutes.

5. Meanwhile, mix the glaze. Add powdered sugar, remaining tbsp of butter, tsp of vanilla or caramel extract, and 2-4 tbsp of milk to a small bowl. Mix until well combined and put aside.

6. When pies are golden brown, remove from oven and let cool for 5 minutes before brushing with glaze. Allow to cool for a few more minutes and add another coat of glaze.

   Enjoy! PS.- Papa likes to serve them over a scoop of vanilla ice cream!

Now it's time for you to go out and plant some seeds of your own!
Planting seeds of kindness can be simple, but here are some ideas to get you started.

1. Bake some yummy treats for a friend or neighbor. (Check out the recipe to the left.)
2. Paint rocks with positive notes and hide them around town.
3. Surprise a friend with a "Celebrate You Day", kind of like a birthday, but completely random.
4. Take a jar of change and fill vending machines, parking meters, or candy machines for people to find.
5. Use sidewalk chalk to create positive messages for all to see.
6. Clean up around your town park, city, or even a neighbor's yard.
7. Read a book to a grandparent or an elderly person at a nursing home.
8. Do a chore for someone in your family.
9. Leave a special gift on someone's doorstep.
10. Be a friend to the new kid.
11. Pay for the person behind you in the drive-thru line.
12. Leave a treat for the mailman.
13. Buy a copy of this book to share with a friend and challenge them to plant some seeds too!
14. Make an inspirational video to share with phone contacts or on social media.
15. Encourage someone.
16. Use your talent to make someone's day!
17. Write a thank you letter to someone who has made a difference in your life.
18. Serve someone else for an entire day.
19. Attach a bag of popcorn and a kind note to a movie kiosk.
20. Make a bookmark with a kind note on it to leave inside a library book before returning it.
21. Hide dollar bills around a store.
22. Donate your gently used toys and clothes.
23. Make someone laugh.
24. Clean your bedroom without being asked.
25. Say thank you to a lunch worker or bus driver.
26. Hold the door open for others.
27. Help a classmate if they are struggling.
28. Write your own positive "pass it on" note.
29. Make cards or treats for your local police department, fire department, or medical workers.
30. Be creative and create your very own seed of kindness to share with the world!

Always remember- a tiny seed can go a long way!

Do you have even more great ideas about how to plant good seeds? I'd love to see them! Ask a parent to post on Facebook or Instagram using the official hashtag #OhTheSeedsYouCanSow. To join the challenge and to grab your free printable, visit www.fromseedstotreespress.com.

Check out the other books in
"The Adventures of Janie Grace"
series here! More titles coming soon!

We'd love to see pictures of your little readers and hear your feedback. Tag us @theadventuresofjaniegrace on Facebook and Instagram, and don't forget to leave a review on Amazon!

Made in the USA
Middletown, DE
26 September 2023

39477958R00018